Nubbin

Saddle Up Series
Book 43

Dave and Pat Sargent are longtime residents of Prairie Grove, Arkansas. Dave, a fourth-generation dairy farmer, began writing in early December 1990. Pat, a former teacher, began writing shortly after. They enjoy the outdoors and have a real love for animals.

Nubbin

Saddle Up Series
Book 43

By Dave and Pat Sargent

Beyond "The End"
By Sue Rogers

Illustrated by Jane Lenoir

Ozark Publishing, Inc.
P.O. Box 228
Prairie Grove, AR 72753

Cataloging-in-Publication Data

Sargent, Dave, 1941–
  Nubbin / by Dave and Pat Sargent ;
illustrated by Jane Lenoir.—Prairie Grove, AR :
Ozark Publishing, c2004.
    p. cm. (Saddle up series ; 43)

  "Freedom"—Cover.
  SUMMARY: Nubbin, a linebacked apricot
dun horse, helps Harriet Tubman escape from a
southern plantation and aids her in her work
with the Underground Railroad. Contains
factual information about linebacked apricot
dun horses.
    ISBN 1-56763-703-5 (hc)
          1-56763-704-3 (pbk)

    1. Horses—Juvenile Fiction. [1. Horses—
Fiction. 2. Tubman, Harriet, 1820?–1913—
Fiction. 3. Underground railroad—Fiction.
4. African Americans—Fiction.] I. Sargent,
Pat, 1936– II. Lenoir, Jane, 1950– ill.
III. Title. IV. Series.
    PZ7.S2465Nu 2004
    [Fic]--dc21   2001005622

Printed in the United States of America

Inspired by

linebacked apricot duns we see as we travel. They are a light color.

Dedicated to

all kids who love to ride horses and love living in this free country.

Foreword

When Harriet Tubman asks Nubbin the linebacked apricot dun to help her escape from a plantation in the south and make her way north, he doesn't hesitate. Harriet Tubman is helpful in the struggle to free slaves, and the linebacked apricot dun works hard, helping her with the Underground Railroad operation.

Contents

If you would like to have the authors of the Saddle Up Series visit your school, free of charge, call 1-800-321-5671 or 1-800-960-3876.

vi

One

Harriet Tubman

The moon was overhead when Nubbin the linebacked apricot dun awoke from a deep sleep. "Hmmm," he thought. "I wonder what it was that woke me up from such a good nap?" He glanced around at the quiet plantation.

"Everybody is sleeping," he muttered. "Maybe I was having a dream and just don't remember it."

"Shhh," a voice hissed from amid the shadows of the trees. "Be real quiet, Nubbin."

The linebacked apricot dun strained to see who was speaking to him. He looked to the right, and then he looked to the left.

"That voice sounds familiar," he murmured. "But it was so low that I can't recognize it."

Suddenly he saw a young lady running quietly through the woods toward him.

"My good friend!" he nickered. "What are you doing up so late?"

"Shhh," Harriet hissed again. "I'm running away, Nubbin, and I need your help."

"Of course I'll help you," he whinnied. "But I don't understand. Why are you running away? I thought you were getting along good for a slave girl."

Harriet leaped on his bare back and whispered, "Go north, Nubbin. Go north until we can't be found by my owner or my husband."

"Okay, Boss," he nickered with a smile. "I'm your horse now. Hang onto my mane, and we'll make fast tracks away from here."

The linebacked apricot dun and his young lady slave boss moved silently through the night. He felt

her body trembling as they lost sight
of the plantation and turned north.

"Don't be frightened," Nubbin whinnied quietly. "I'll protect you."

Harriet chuckled softly and said, "For goodness' sake, Nubbin. Just look at me quiver and shake. Why, a person would think that I was scared to death."

"Well," Nubbin muttered, "I don't know what a person might think, but this linebacked apricot dun horse sure thought you were scared."

"I'm excited," she murmured. "I'm excited about being free, and I'm excited about following my dream to help other slaves escape from bondage. And," she added with a nervous giggle, "I'm happy to be rid of that John Tubman husband of mine!"

"Hmmm," Nubbin thought as he stopped to rest for a few minutes.

"She must not like her husband very much."

As she slid off his back, Harriet said, "I didn't want to marry him. My owner made me do it."

Suddenly, she squealed and started dancing around Nubbin.

"Oh dear," Nubbin groaned. "My poor boss has lost her mind."

"I am free," Harriet Tubman sang softly. "I'm free from everyone and everything that I don't like." She grabbed Nubbin around his neck and hugged him. "Now you and I can help my people to freedom."

As she released him and started dancing again, Nubbin smiled and tapped one hoof upon the ground. A short time later, Harriet fell onto the grass, laughing and chattering happily.

"In 1821, Nubbin, I was born into slavery in Dorchester County, Maryland," she confided. "Folks back then named me Araminta, but I didn't like the name so I changed it to Harriet. I like the name Harriet much better, don't you, Nubbin?"

Nubbin nickered and nodded his head. "I like the name of Harriet, Boss. It fits you real good."

The linebacked apricot dun and the young black lady rested beside a stream for nearly an hour.

As the sun slowly crept above the eastern horizon, Nubbin took a short nap. But Harriet was like a small child seeing the world for the very first time. For a little while, she watched a fish swimming in the cool water, and then she picked a small bouquet of wildflowers.

A butterfly suddenly captured Harriet's attention as it fluttered near a blossom. Her girlish giggle woke Nubbin, and he had to smile as he watched her enjoying the wonders of nature. It was as if she were seeing these things for the very first time.

A sudden nicker from a horse and the loud voices of men captured Nubbin and Harriet's attention.

"That little slave gal couldn't have traveled this far," a gruff voice boomed.

"Nope," another voice agreed. "She doesn't have a horse or buggy or anything. I reckon we need to turn around and check where we've already been. That gal was probably hiding in the woods when we went by."

As the search party turned around, their voices faded away. A moment later, Harriet again hugged Nubbin's neck.

"I wouldn't be able to escape, Nubbin, without your help."

He nickered softly and nuzzled her on her cheek with his lip.

"Don't worry, Boss," he said. "We'll be in north country real soon, and you'll be safe from harm."

Two

Escape to Freedom

The linebacked apricot dun and the slave girl traveled by night and rested, hidden away, by day. Almost a week following their successful escape from the big plantation, they once again stopped to rest as the sun peeked over the eastern horizon. The horse and rider were exhausted from both fast and vigilant travel.

Harriet slipped from Nubbin's back and curled up on the soft grass. And a moment later, she was sound asleep.

The linebacked apricot dun yawned as he carefully checked the area for anything that could possibly be a danger to his boss.

"Hmmm," he murmured as he returned. "Perhaps I'd better get some rest, too. This seems to be a safe place to do it."

Within seconds, he was snoring gently.

"Shhh."

The familiar hiss echoed within the dream that Nubbin was seeing in his mind.

"Don't wake them," a voice whispered. "They look exhausted."

Nubbin gently shook his head and then opened his eyes.

He snorted and gasped, "Uh-oh! You better wake up, Boss. We have company."

Three men were standing near Harriet.

"Boss," Nubbin neighed loudly. "Wake up!"

Boss Harriet sat straight up and rubbed her eyes.

"Nubbin," she scolded. "What in the world is the matter with..." She blinked as she stared at the men. "Uh-oh," she murmured quietly.

"Don't be frightened, little gal," one of the men said. "We're going to help you."

"Huh?" Nubbin gasped. "Help my boss? What are you going to do? Take her back to the plantation and her owner and a husband she hates?" His ears flattened against his head and he snorted, "No, you aren't. Don't worry, Boss. I'll save you."

He whirled into the swift kick position and backed up two paces.

"Where are we?" Harriet asked the men.

Nubbin backed up two more paces, taking aim.

"You're in New York," another man replied. "You're safe now."

Nubbin was raising one hind foot when his boss yelled, "No!"

The three men flinched.

"Yes," one of the men said in a soothing voice as he stooped down beside her. "It's true. You're safe with us. Don't be afraid."

Nubbin put his foot back on the ground and waited.

Harriet took a deep breath then smiled and looked at her horse.

"I'm not afraid anymore," she said cheerfully.

"That's good," the man said. "Let's go get you some hot food and a roof over your head, young lady. You need a rest after your long hard journey to freedom from slavery."

"That sounds so wonderful," Harriet murmured. "Thank you."

"Humph," Nubbin snorted. "And what about me? Might I have some oats and fresh hay?"

The group traveled for several hours en route to their destination. Nubbin listened to Harriet and the men visit as they moved through the countryside, heading for Auburn, New York. The men told her of national unrest about slavery and spoke of something that was being called the Underground Railroad.

"Hmmm," Nubbin murmured. "I've seen railroads, but I wonder how they get those trains to travel under the ground. Wow! I guess the United States is coming up with new things every day." A short time later, they entered the town.

The linebacked apricot dun smiled and nickered. "I like the looks of our new home. But," he added, "any place that makes Boss this happy is perfect for me!"

A grey sabino was standing at a hitching post as they passed.

He nickered, "Hello, stranger. Welcome to Auburn."

"Why, thanks," Nubbin said with a friendly smile. "I sure like your town, Grey Sabino."

The grey sabino pawed the ground with one hoof and nodded his head.

"It's a happy and safe place to live," he said proudly. "Here in Auburn, we are trying to help free the slaves."

"Wonderful!" Nubbin nickered. "Boss and I will help with that plan. You can count on that."

Three

The Underground Railroad

Exactly one week later, Nubbin was relaxing in the pasture when he saw Harriet running toward him.

"What's the matter, Boss?" he nickered as he ran to meet her.

He breathed a big sigh of relief when he saw that she was smiling.

"Nubbin, I have exciting news," she said.

"That's great!" he neighed. "What's happening, Boss?"

"I'm going to work with the Underground Railroad," she stated.

"Oh boy," Nubbin groaned
aloud. "I don't think you should be
traveling the rails under the ground,
Boss. But if you insist on doing it,
I'll help you."

"The Underground Railroad is a series of folks who help slaves escape from bondage," Harriet explained. "You and I will help my folks reach freedom. And Quaker sympathizers are going to help us bring them north, Nubbin."

"Hmmm," Nubbin nickered. "That sounds good. And I'm sure relieved to know that we can walk on top of the ground instead of, uh, the other way."

And so, for eight years or so, Nubbin and Harriet rescued slaves. They went on over twenty missions, and every one was dangerous. The linebacked apricot dun watched his boss with pride, yet feared for her safety. His main job was to keep his boss safe from harm as she freed slave after slave from bondage.

One evening in 1857, Harriet confided that they were going on an extra special mission.

"Nubbin," she said quietly, "every slave is important to me."

"I know that, Boss," he said with a nod of his head. "You care about everybody."

Suddenly a tear trickled down her cheek. Nubbin groaned, and a tear fell from the corner of his eye.

"What's the matter, Boss?" he whinnied. "Why do you feel so sad? I thought we were doing a good job with the Underground Railroad."

Harriet hugged him before whispering, "Tomorrow we're going to try to free my mother and father." Then she said with a little groan, "Nubbin, I would just die if we failed on this mission."

"We'll not fail, Boss," Nubbin said in a firm voice. "We're good at what we do. We'll get your mama and daddy and bring them back to Auburn."

And sure enough, ten days later, the linebacked apricot dun, his very determined and happy lady boss, and her mother and father, who were very grateful, all entered the safe haven of Auburn, New York.

As they stopped in front of the new home Harriet had acquired for her parents, her father said, "I truly believe there will be a war one day soon, Harriet."

"Uh-huh," Nubbin nickered. "The North and the South disagree on slavery."

"War is always a terrible thing," Harriet said. "But slavery should be abolished, and I intend to help the fight for freedom." She smiled at her father and added, "But we won't worry about that right now."

"Good!" Nubbin said with a whinny. "Today we must celebrate the rescue of your parents from bondage, Boss. Tomorrow is a new and promising day for all of us."

As his boss and her parents walked toward their new home,

Nubbin nodded his head. "Hmmm," he thought. "I believe my lady boss, Harriet Tubman, will be remembered in American history books for her role in helping free slaves."

"But," he murmured softly, "I wonder if folks will remember her linebacked apricot dun named Nubbin." He shook his head and added, "It doesn't matter. My life is one great big exciting adventure!"

Four

Linebacked Apricot Dun Facts

The term *dun* is used by cowboys to indicate yellow horses with black points, but it can also describe the lighter colors of horses that may or may not have black points.

Duns with no black points include red duns and yellow duns. The red dun group includes the apricot duns. A black stripe down the apricot dun's back makes that horse a linebacked apricot dun. It is the lighter color of the red dun group.

Linebacked Apricot Dun

BEYOND "THE END"

To ride a horse is to fly without wings.
Anonymous

WORD LIST

Maryland	New York
nuzzle	white stocking
grey sabino	white coronet
nicker	strawberry roan
palomino	white heel
snort	piebald
kick	Thoroughbred
white sock	snore
paw	linebacked apricot dun

From the word list on page 37, write:

1. Six words that tell things horses do.

2. Four words that tell leg markings on a horse. Draw four horse legs and show each marking.

3. Two words that are states in the United States. Why are these two states important in this story?

4. One word that names a breed of horse.

5. Five words that tell the color of horses. Chapter Four gives a description of a linebacked apricot dun. Describe the other four horse colors.

CURRICULUM CONNECTIONS

What was the Underground Railroad that Harriet Tubman and others operated? What was the importance of spirituals? Who were conductors and what did they do?

There is a great website that answers these questions and furnishes more interesting information. A second-grade class in New York established it after the students studied about Harriet Tubman. Look at <www2.lhric.org/pocantico/tubman/tubman.html>.

There was probably plenty of grass for Nubbin to eat along the journey as he and Harriet Tubman dashed for freedom, but he needed salt also. How do you suppose Nubbin or Harriet found salt for him? What do you think Harriet ate? She was riding bareback so there were no saddlebags to store supplies!

Write a short story, poem, or song that tells how Harriet must have felt watching a fish swimming in the cool water, or picking a bouquet of wildflowers, or watching a butterfly fluttering by.

PROJECT

Combine your math and artistic skills! Draw to scale and accurately color a picture (body, tail, and mane) of the horse that is featured in each book read in the Saddle Up Series. You could soon have sixty horses prancing around the walls of your classroom!

Learning + horses = FUN.

Look in your school library media center for books about how to draw a horse and the colors of horses. Don't forget the useful information in the last chapter of this book (Linebacked Apricot Dun Facts) and the picture on the book cover for a shape and color guide.

HELPFUL HINTS AND WEBSITES

A horse is measured in hands. One hand equals four inches. Use a scale of 1" equals 1 hand.

Visit website <www.equisearch.com> to find a glossary of equine terms, information about tack and equipment, breeds, art and graphics, and more about horses. Learn more at <www.horse-country. com> and at <www.ansi.okstate.edu/ breeds/horses/>.

KidsClick! is a web search for kids by librarians. There are many interesting websites here. HORSES and HORSE-MANSHIP are two of the more than 600 subjects. Visit <www.kidsclick.org>.

Is your classroom beginning to look like the Rocking S Horse Ranch? Happy Trails to You!